Rosie ᴬɴᴅ Michael

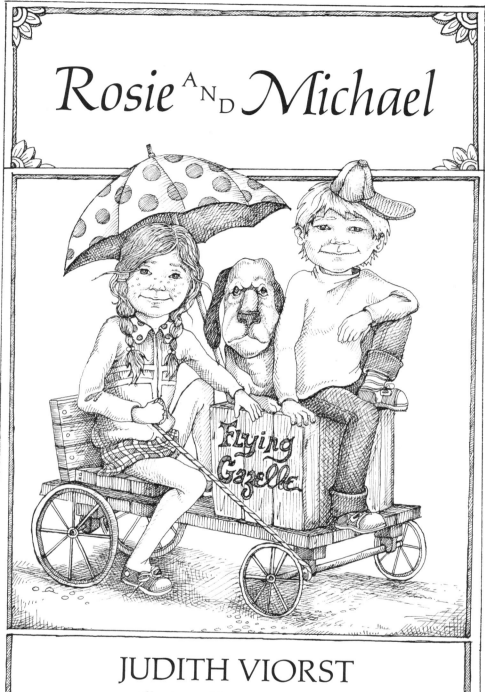

JUDITH VIORST

Illustrated by Lorna Tomei

Atheneum New York

Atheneum
Macmillan Publishing Company
866 Third Avenue, New York, NY 10022
Collier Macmillan Canada, Inc.

Manufactured in the United States of America
Printed by Halliday Lithograph Corporation
Bound by A. Horowitz & Son/Bookbinders
Clifton, New Jersey

First Edition

13   15   17   19   20   18   16   14   12

Library of Congress Catalog card
number: 74-75571
ISBN 0-689-30439-0

For Sheila King Clarke, a special friend

Rosie is my friend.

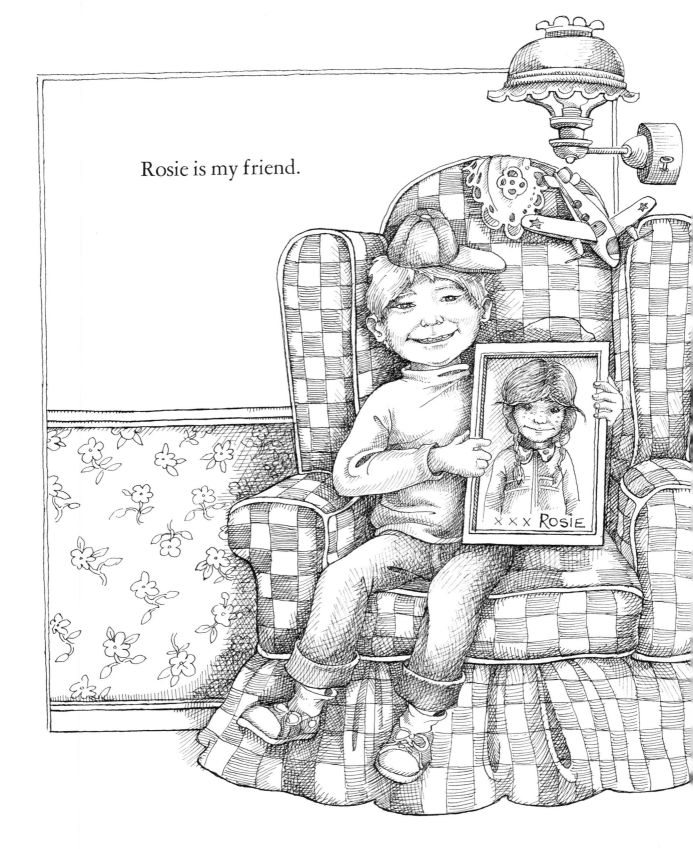

She likes me when I'm dopey and not just when I'm
smart.

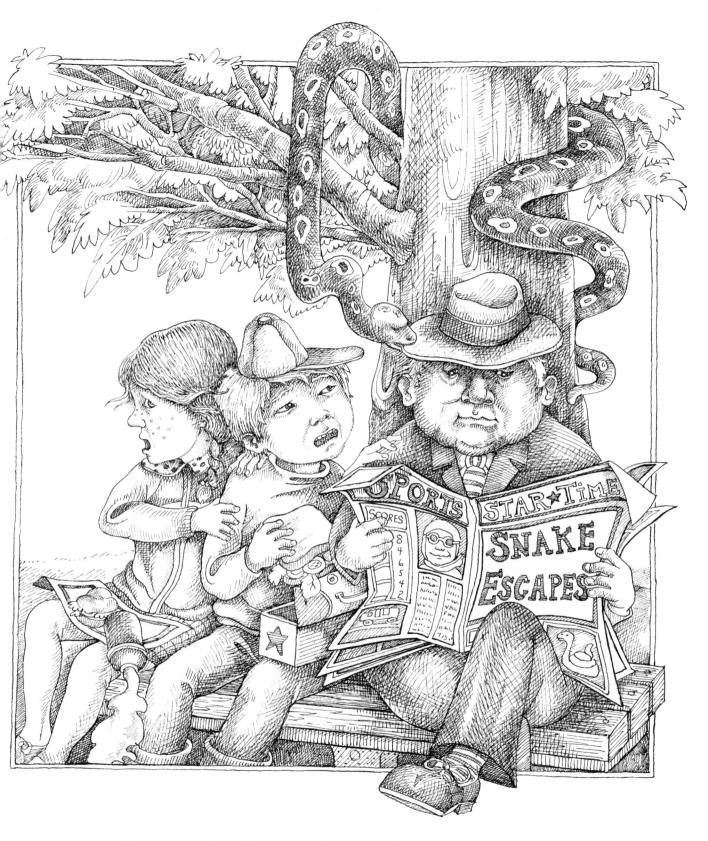

I worry a lot about pythons, and she understands.

My toes point in,
and my shoulders droop,
and there's hair growing
out of my ears.

But Rosie says I look good.

She is my friend.

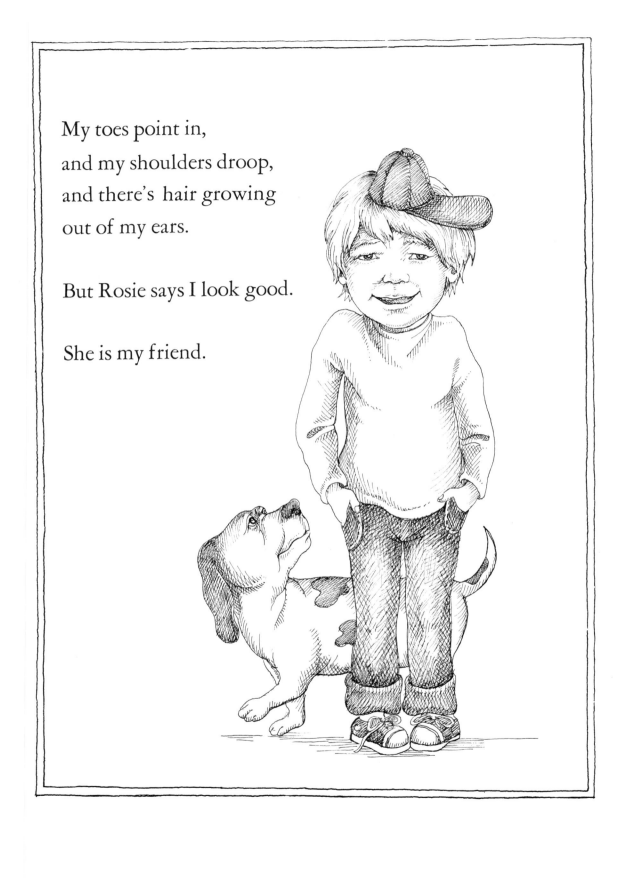

Michael is my friend.

He likes me when I'm grouchy
and not just when I'm nice.

I worry a lot about were-
wolves, and he understands.
There's freckles growing all
over me, except on my eye-
balls and teeth.

But Michael says I look good.

He is my friend.

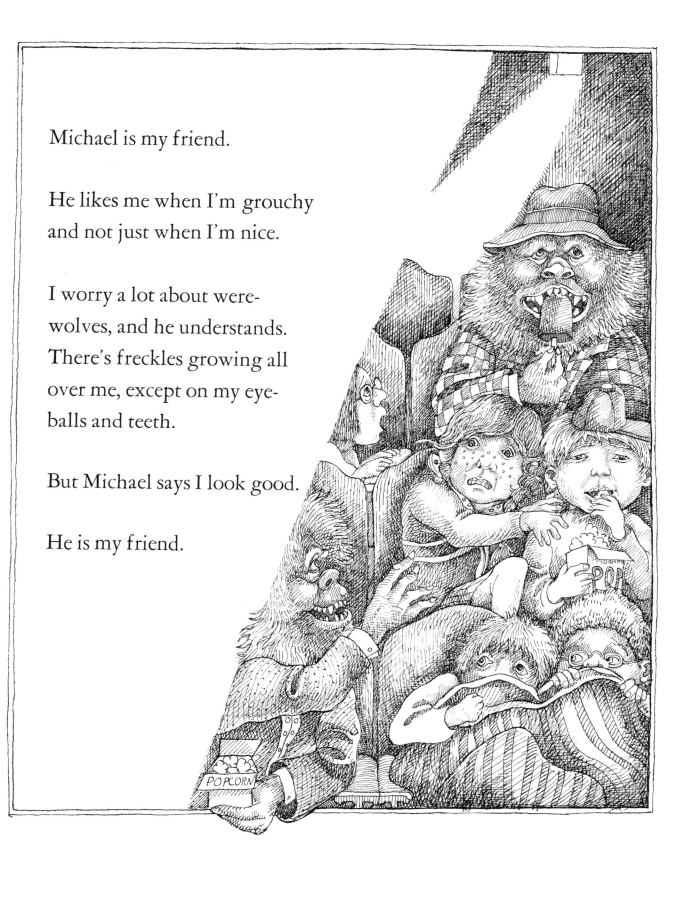

When I said that my nickname was Mickey, Rosie said Mickey. When I said that my nickname was Ace, Rosie said Ace. And when I was Tiger, and Lefty, and Ringo, Rosie always remembered.

That's how friends are.

When I wrote my name with a *y,* Michael wrote Rosey. When I wrote my name with an *i,* Michael wrote Rosi. And when I wrote Rosee, and Rozi, and Wrosie, Michael always did too.

That's how friends are.

Just because I sprayed Kool Whip in her sneakers,
doesn't mean that Rosie's not my friend.

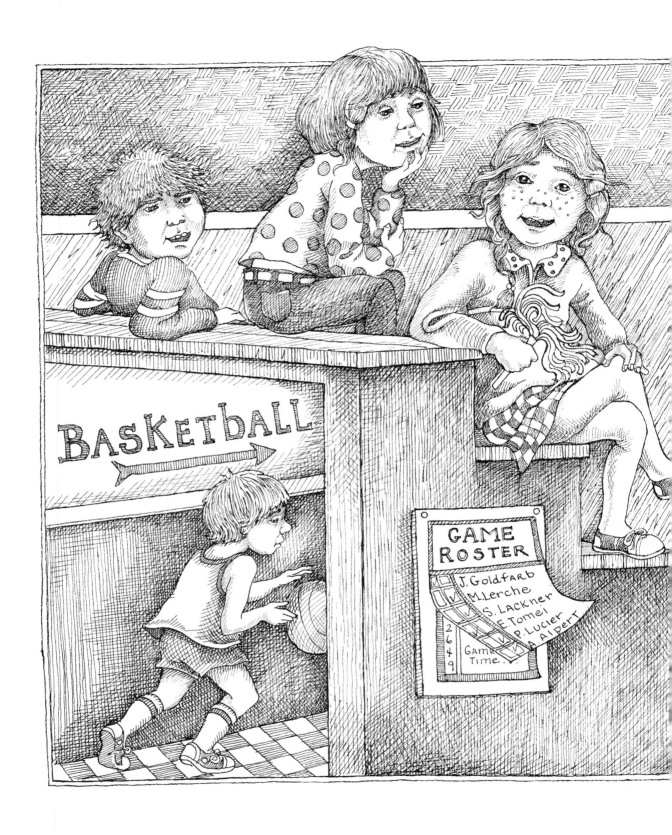

Just because I let the air out of his basketball, doesn't mean that Michael's not my friend.

When my parakeet died, I called Rosie.

When my bike got swiped, I called Rosie.

When I cut my head and the blood came
gushing out, as soon as the blood stopped
gushing, I called Rosie.

She is my friend.

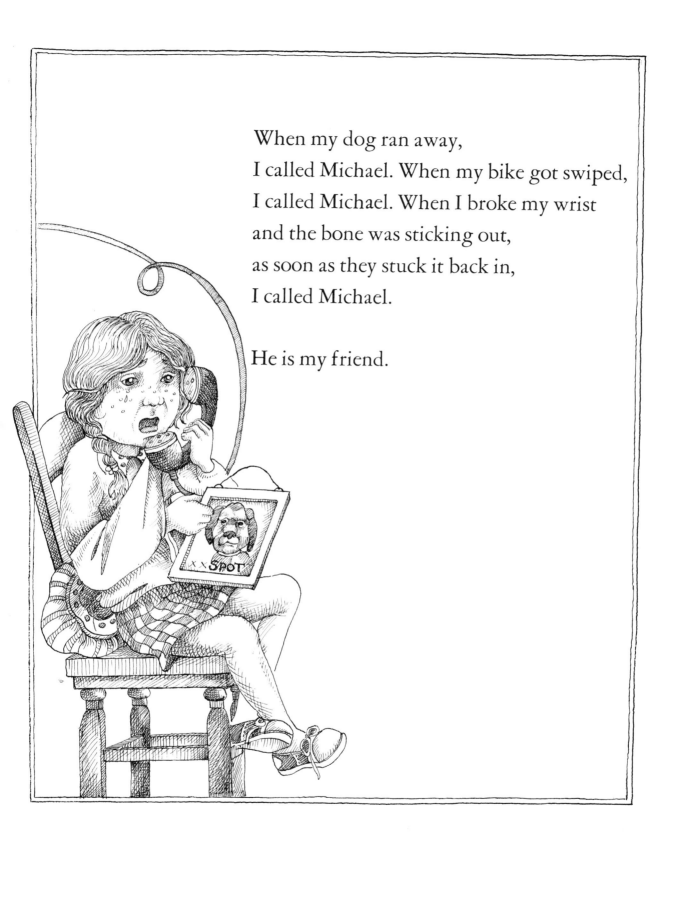

When my dog ran away,
I called Michael. When my bike got swiped,
I called Michael. When I broke my wrist
and the bone was sticking out,
as soon as they stuck it back in,
I called Michael.

He is my friend.

It wouldn't matter if two billion people said she robbed a bank.

If Rosie told me she didn't, I'd believe her.

Even though his fingerprints
were found all over the
dagger, if Michael said, "I'm
innocent," I'd believe him.

Just because I dug a
hole and covered it with

leaves and told her to
jump on the leaves

and she fell in the hole, doesn't mean that Rosie's not my friend.

Just because I put a worm in his tuna salad sandwich,
doesn't mean that Michael's not my friend.

Rosie is my friend. I sold her my yo-yo that glows in
the dark for only fifty cents. I would have charged
Alvin Alpert seventy-five.

Michael is my friend. I traded him my whiffle bat for
only fourteen marbles. It would have been twenty
marbles for Alvin Alpert.

If Rosie told me a secret and people hit me and bit me, I wouldn't tell what Rosie's secret was. And then if people twisted my arm and kicked me in the shins, I still wouldn't tell what Rosie's secret was. And then if people said, "Speak up, or we'll throw you in this quicksand," Rosie would forgive me for telling her secret.

If Michael told me a
secret and people
clonked me and bopped
me, I wouldn't tell
what Michael's secret
was. And then if people
bent back my fingers
and wrestled me to the
ground, I still wouldn't
tell what Michael's
secret was.

And then if people said,
"Speak up, or we'll feed
you to these piranhas,"
Michael would forgive
me for telling his secret.

Just because I call her a

GORILLA

FACE

doesn't mean that
Rosie's not my friend.

Just because I call him a

doesn't mean that
Michael's not my friend.

Sometimes I get on the diving board and decide that
I've changed my mind. But Rosie wouldn't laugh.
She is my friend.

Sometimes I'm climbing up a tree and decide that
I'd rather climb down. But Michael wouldn't laugh.
He is my friend.

If Rosie bought me an ice-cream bar, it wouldn't be toasted almond. If Rosie bought me a shirt, it wouldn't be green. If Rosie bought me a book, it wouldn't be *How Your Sewer System Works,* or *Sven of Sweden.*

You can count on a friend.

If Michael bought me some candy, it wouldn't be licorice. If Michael bought me a scarf, it wouldn't be brown. If Michael bought me a book, it wouldn't be *Know Your Lungs,* or *Dances of Costa Rica.*

You can count on a friend.

Even though I was voted Most Horrible Singing Voice
in the Class, Rosie says that Alvin Alpert sings worse.

Even though I was voted Bossiest Person in the Class,
Michael says that Alvin Alpert is bossier.

Rosie is my friend. When she honest and truly wanted to know if she walked like a kangaroo, I honestly told her.

Michael is my friend. When he honest and truly wanted to know if his feet were smelling stinky, I honestly told him.

Rosie would try to save me if there was a tidal wave.

She'd hunt for me if kidnappers stole me away.

And if I never was found again, she could have my Instamatic. She is my friend.

Michael would try to save me
if a lion attacked.

He'd catch me if I jumped
from a burning house.

And if by mistake he missed the catch, he could have my
stamp collection.   He is my friend.

I'd never get my tonsils out if Rosie didn't, too.

I'd never move to China without Michael.

I'd give her my last piece of chalk.
I'd give him my last Chicklet.
Rosie is
Michael is
My friend.